For Coral

MYRIAD BOOKS LIMITED
35 Bishopsthorpe Road, London SE26 4PA

First published in 2005 by
PICCADILLY PRESS LIMITED
5 Castle Road, London NW1 8PR
www.piccadillypress.co.uk

ISBN 1 905606 97 4
EAN 9 781905 606 979

Designed by Simon Davis

Printed in China

A true story!
When I lived in Malaysia, I saw a tiny ball of fluff for sale in a market. The animal looked so small
and helpless that I rescued it, and it turned out to be a baby river otter. We fed it with powdered
milk five times a day and gradually Oscar grew into a fine, healthy young otter, with whom we had
many adventures. Like all young children, Oscar had to learn everything,
including how to swim. This book came about from remembering all those happy times!

- Adrienne Kennaway

An Otter's First Swim

Adrienne Kennaway

MYRIAD BOOKS LIMITED

Late one morning, when the tide was low, a mother otter led her three cubs over the rocks and the seaweed to the shoreline.

"You've been bobbing about in the shallows, but it is time now for your first swimming lesson in deep water," she said. "You'll love swimming."

She dived in and splashed them playfully.

"Come in, the water's lovely," she whistled happily.

The little otters
weren't so certain.

She picked up the first little otter, and carried her
into the sea, where – with a little help –

soon she was playing and swimming.

The second little otter thought it looked
like fun, and dived in before
his mother came back.

He learned quickly too, and floated, swam and played with his
sister and mother.

The third little otter stayed behind.

His sister and brother
whistled to him to join them.

"Come on, it's lovely!" they called.

But when the cold water splashed against
him, he sprang back. It was cold and horrid!

There was *no way* he was
going into that water!

He trotted away from the
sea as fast as his little legs
would carry him.

His mother whistled and called
after him, but he didn't turn around.

He climbed on to a rock, and decided
to lie in the sun for a while to catch his breath.
Before he knew it, he was yawning, and
shortly after that he was fast asleep . . .

He woke with a start to the sound of piercing whistles. His family were trying to get his attention. The tide had turned and the sea was rising quickly all around his rock.

The little otter stood up
and looked around
anxiously for another rock
to jump on to. But he was

TRAPPED!

The water was getting higher and higher, and the other otters swam around, shouting for him to jump in. But he didn't want to go in, and he didn't know what to do.

Soon, there was only one thing he could do . . .

... SPLASH!

He was in the water and sinking to the bottom.

"*Swim up, up . . . .*"
his mother said. She was
right behind him, guiding
him towards the surface.

As they reached the surface, she said,
"Now breathe," and showed him how.

And to the little otter's surprise,
now that he was swimming,
he found pleasure in
the cool water.

Soon he was diving for fish,

chasing his mother,

and playing with his brother and sister.

He had so much fun that he didn't realise that the hours were passing, and . . .

. . . soon it was time to go home!

Otter Facts

There are thirteen species of otter
throughout the world. This story
is about an Eurasian otter,
the only otter native to the UK.

Where are they found?

Eurasian otters live throughout
Europe, right up to the Arctic
Circle and all over most of Asia
and northern Africa. They are often
confused with sea otters, which tend
to be bigger and heavier and are found
along the Pacific coast of North America.

Eurasian otters live by lakes, rivers,
marshes and along rocky coastlines.
They make mossy dens under rocks and tree
roots. These dens are called holts.

What do they eat?

They hunt for fish and crabs and use rocks
as tools to break open shellfish. On dry
land they search for frogs, birds and
small mammals. Their sensitive
whiskers and keen sense of smell
help them to find food.

Swimming

When the cubs are about three months old, their mother takes them to the water. They are often frightened of the water and it can take her several days to coax them in. At first they simply float and bob around, but when they are about four months old, they have their first dive.

Once they learn, they become exceptional swimmers. They have two layers of fur (a thick, waterproof outer layer and a warm, inner one), webbed toes and a rudder-like tail to help them move faster in the water. They can even close their ears and nostrils while underwater and they hold their breath for about twenty seconds.

Otters in danger

In many countries, otters have become extinct or endangered because of pollution and hunting. Conservationists are helping to save wild otters. To support or find out more about otter conservation contact:

The International Otter Survival Fund: www.otter.org
WWF: www.wwf.org.uk
The Otter Trust: www.ottertrust.org.uk